Alfie's Feet

Other Picture Books by
SHIRLEY HUGHES

Alfie Gets in First
Alfie Gives a Hand
The Big Alfie and Annie Rose Storybook
Dogger
(Winner of the 1977 Kate Greenaway Medal)
An Evening at Alfie's
Helpers
*(Highly commended for the 1975 Kate Greenaway
Medal and Winner of the 1976 Other Award)*
Moving Molly
Sally's Secret
Up and Up

*For
Edward and Catherine*

British Library Cataloguing in Publication Data
Hughes, Shirley   Alfie's Feet
I. Title 823'914 [J] PZ7   ISBN 0–370–30416–0
Copyright © Shirley Hughes 1982   Printed in Great Britain for
The Bodley Head Ltd, 32 Bedford Square, London WC1B 3SG
by W. S. Cowell Ltd, Ipswich
First published 1982   Reprinted 1983, 1986, 1989

Alfie's Feet
Shirley Hughes

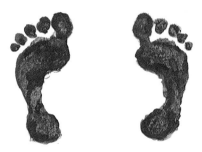

THE BODLEY HEAD

London

This little pig went to market,

This little pig stayed at home,

This little pig had roast beef,

This little pig had none,

And this little pig cried, Wee-wee-wee-wee-wee,

I can't find my way home.

Alfie had a little sister called Annie Rose.
Alfie's feet were quite big. Annie Rose's feet
were rather small. They were all soft and pink
underneath. Alfie knew a game he could play
with Annie Rose, counting her toes.

Annie Rose had lots of different ways of getting about. She went forwards, crawling,

and backwards, on her behind,

and she liked to slide about very fast on her potty,

skidding round and round
on the floor and in and out
of the table legs.

Annie Rose had
some new red shoes.

She could walk in them
a bit, if she was pushing her
little cart or holding on to
someone's hand.

When they went out, Annie Rose wore her
red shoes and Alfie wore his old brown ones.
Mum usually helped him put them on, because
he wasn't very good at doing up the laces yet.

If it had been raining Alfie
liked to go stamping about in
mud and walking through puddles,

splish, splash, SPLOSH!

Then his shoes got rather wet.

So did his socks,

and so did his feet.

So one Saturday morning Alfie and Mum went to a big shop in the High Street.

They bought a pair of shiny new yellow boots for Alfie to wear when he went stamping about in mud and walking through puddles. Alfie was very pleased. He carried them home himself in a cardboard box.

When they got in, Alfie sat down at once and unwrapped his new boots. He put them on all by himself and walked about in them,

stamp! stamp! stamp!

He went into the kitchen to show Mum and Dad
and Annie Rose, stamping his feet all the way,

stamp! stamp! stamp!

The boots were very smart
and shiny but they felt funny.

Alfie wanted to go out again right away. So he put on his mac, and Dad took his book and his newspaper and they went off to the park.

Alfie stamped in a lot of mud and walked through a lot of puddles, splish, splash, SPLOSH! He frightened some sparrows who were having a bath. He even frightened two big ducks. They went hurrying back to their pond, walking with their feet turned in.

Alfie looked down at his feet. They still
felt funny. They kept turning outwards.
Dad was sitting on a bench. They both
looked at Alfie's feet.

Suddenly Alfie knew what was wrong!

Dad lifted Alfie on to the bench beside him and helped him to take off each boot and put it on the other foot. And when Alfie stood down again his feet didn't feel a bit funny any more.

After tea Mum painted a big black R on to one of Alfie's boots and a big black L on the other to help Alfie remember which boot was which. The R was for Right foot and the L was for Left foot. The black paint wore off in the end and the boots stopped being new and shiny, but Alfie usually did remember to get them on the proper way round after that. They felt much better when he went stamping about in mud and walking through puddles.

And, of course, Annie Rose made such a fuss about Alfie having new boots that she had to have a pair of her own to go stamping about in too, splish, splash, SPLOSH!